THE LAVENDER SEMAPHORE

ADELAIDE BECKET – STORY 4

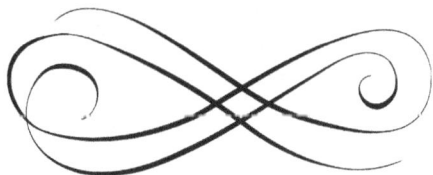

Published by Stories Rule Press Inc.
Edmonton, Alberta, Canada.

Registered offices:
1100-10020 101A Avenue NW
Edmonton AB T5J 3G2
Canada

This is an original work by Tracy Cooper-Posey
Copyright © 2021

FIRST EDITION: July 2021

Tracy Cooper-Posey
The Lavender Semaphore/Tracy Cooper-Posey—1st Ed.

Historical—Fiction
Suspense—Fiction

IngramSpark ISBN: 9781774384749
Amazon KDP Print ISBN: 9781774384695

Praise for the Adelaide Becket series

Tracy takes you again back in time to an era you could only imagine about but brings it in vivid color through her story

A delightful game of cat and mouse

I thoroughly enjoyed this magnificent first in series book!!

The writing style is easy to read and the plot COMPLETELY unpredictable!!

It was a marvelous escape from reality

Breathtaking start to a fantastic new series by Tracy Cooper-Posey.

Succinct and yet rich in the details that create historical immersion and scenes I found easy to imagine being a part.

I loooove good quality writing and I love a new series like a junkie. Just give it a try, you won't be disappointed!

The Story So Far…

The first three stories in this series are The Requisite Courage, The Rosewater Debutante *and* The Unaccompanied Widow. *If you have not yet read the preceding stories in this series, this summary will reveal spoilers.*

Lady Adelaide Azalea Margaret de Morville, Mrs. Hugh Becket, lived in the Cape Colony with her commoner husband for eight years. There, she learned to speak and read German. Adele was widowed in a tragic accident and returned to London in early 1906.

William Melville, a former Scotland Yard senior official and now a shadowy figure in the British government, recruits Adele to help him uncover German agents in Britain, who seek to weaken the Empire. Adele also meets Daniel Hargrave Bannister II, Baron Leighton, whom Melville also employs.

While Adele learns how to operate in Melville's shadowy world, she foils a German conspiracy surrounding King Edward at Balmoral, uncovers an agent among Britain's peerage and recruits the Fenian and intellectual, Torin Slane, to work for Melville, too. Adele is growing comfortable with the strange world she has stepped into, until it clashes with her former life...

Now read on.

The Lavender Semaphore

Queens Street, Mayfair. September 8, 1907.

At first, Adele thought a homeless waif had used her kitchen door as a bed. She had slept late because of the previous evening's events, and was still barely awake when she slipped down to the kitchen just past nine o'clock in the morning. The cathedral and church bells had fallen mercifully silent, although they had stirred her enough she could not simply turn over and go back to sleep.

She took off the bar to the outer door, intending to collect the day's milk bottle from the step. She turned the handle, and the door whooshed inward, pushed by a weight against it.

The weight fell onto the painted concrete floor, making Adele gasp and step back, pulling her peignoir hem out of the way. The small child had been curled up, his dirty shoulder against the door. Now he lay on the concrete, blinking up at Adele through sleep-fogged eyes, his face dirt-smeared. He smelled of dampness and desperate circumstances. Adele realized that even though she knew the boy, and he had propped himself against her door for a reason other than sleep, in one respect there was, indeed, a homeless lad using her doorstep as a very uncomfortable mattress.

"Charlie Rowbottom, what *are* you doing, sleeping there?" she demanded.

Charlie rubbed his eyes, which merely redistributed the dirt around them. "I woz 'oping you'd read this to me, tell me if it's werf anyfing." He held up a scrap of paper in his other fist. "Figured it might be werf a bit o' milk, maybe." He looked up at her with large blue eyes and blinked.

Adele tried to harden her heart against such blatant manipulation, but failed. "Oh, get up off the floor, you fool of a child. Come in and tell me about it."

Charlie grinned and scrambled to his feet.

ADELE POURED CHARLIE A GLASS of milk from the new bottle she retrieved from the other side of the step Charlie had been sitting upon. She considered it a small miracle the bottle had still been there, and untouched.

Then, because the small glass of milk disappeared almost instantly, Adele added a hunk of cheese to a bread plate, then hacked off two thick slices of bread from yesterday's loaf. She refilled the milk glass. Charlie set to with gusto.

Adele didn't try to interrupt his meal. Instead, she got the stove burning, made herself a pot of tea and toasted another slice of bread over the flames. She put the butter and a pot of marmalade on the worktable between the two of them, drew her peignoir in around her and settled on the other chair.

Charlie burped and reached eagerly for the marmalade.

She rested a finger on the lid of the pot, holding it down. "Now you say 'pardon me'."

"Pardon *moi.*" He tilted his head, smiling impishly.

Adele estimated that he was around ten years of age, and a small, delicate ten, at that. But he was quick and smart, and if he'd been granted an education, she was sure he would have succeeded magnificently.

He had no parents and could only remember his mother in the vaguest of terms. His little sister had died of tuberculosis a year ago, while confined to a sanitorium. Visiting her there had sufficiently demonstrated to Charlie that any form of authority was not to be trusted, and institutions were to be avoided at all costs. Adele had only suggested once that he might be more comfortable in an orphanage. His derision, and the fear driving it, had left him trembling. She hadn't spoken of it again.

Charlie liked to sleep in Spa Fields, in Clerkenwell. "Softer dirt," he'd observed with appalling practicality. Where he spent the rest of his day was dictated by the police constabulary's routines and where the pickings were richest, which was how Charlie had first come to Adele's attention.

He had attempted to filch her purse from inside her reticule—while she was carrying it, while strolling in Hyde Park. She had grabbed his wrist, made him drop the purse and, because she was offended by his thinness, she had marched him back to her house to feed him. She had wondered if she was setting herself up to become the child's sole source of nourishment. Adele had watched him gobble down the remains of the meat pie from her supper, his other hand curved protectively around the plate, and decided it would not be such a terrible thing to have to provide for him from now on.

But Charlie was too afraid of grown-ups, even those who fed him. He had not returned until many weeks later, when early winter gripped the city with icy fingers. He did not come empty-handed, either. He had held out half-a-dozen leeks, with dirt still clinging to them. The Lord knew which private garden he'd dug them up from. Adele had taken them, then insisted she pay him in kind, and made him sit and eat everything she could find in her kitchen to spare.

She had fed Charlie several times since, always after accepting whatever payment he had managed to scrounge up. He had survived the winter. Summer had come and was now going. But another winter lay just around the corner.

Adele let go of the marmalade. "Tell me about the paper you found," she said, as Charlie used his fingers to dig the marmalade out of the pot. She picked up her knife, took the pot from him and showed him how to spread the marmalade on his bread.

"The paper's got writing all over it." Charlie dug into his trouser pocket and withdrew the paper once more and put it on the table beside his bread plate.

"May I look at it?" she asked, and returned his slice of bread to his plate.

He nodded, took a huge bite out of the bread and chewed.

Adele wiped her fingers on a napkin, and picked up the note. It was a narrow strip of paper and had curled up on itself in a loose scroll. It had been crumpled from Charlie's pocket, but it did not have any sharp folds in it.

She spread the note out, turned it around so the handwriting was the right way up, and examined it. The letters had been written in normal black ink, with a broad nib.

Sehr geehrte Frau Dr, the note began.

Adele drew in a sharp breath. She attempted to cover up the telling sound by stirring on her chair and looking at the note from several different angles, while her heart thudded heavily.

There was only one more line, and it was not German, as the salutation was. It was not English, either. It was an unbroken line of letters. Quite ordinary letters, but they made no sense whatsoever.

"Charlie, where did you get this?" She tried to sound unconcerned.

Charlie lowered the bread, wariness building in his face. "Nowhere."

"You certainly didn't pick this up on the street. It's far too clean. And it wasn't in an envelope, for it hasn't been folded. It has been rolled, instead. I can't think of a single situation where a note of this kind would be rolled and left out where just anyone could come across it."

Charlie shrugged, his gaze on the knife as he dropped marmalade onto his second slice of bread.

"Charlie, this is important," Adele said. "The note..." She hesitated. "You *must* tell me, Charlie. It's possible that...well, you may have stumbled into some trouble over it."

Charlie's gaze met hers. He understood trouble. Then he shook his head. "Nah, no bother'll come of it. It was in a milk bottle, see?"

She sat back. "A milk bottle?"

He nodded, chewing quickly. "Funny sort of milk bottle, too. Thought it was full, 'til I took the lid off. Blasted thing was empty."

That was why he'd tried to sell the note for milk. He'd thought he'd successfully stolen someone else's milk from a milk bottle holder sitting on a doorstep.

"The inside was painted, to look like milk?" Adele asked, keeping her tone light.

Charlie nodded again. "Note was inside it. You like funny stuff, 'n you can read, so..."

She kept her gaze on the note. "And it was the only full bottle in the holder? The other bottles were empty?"

"That's why I took it. You know somethin' about this, then?"

"I'm guessing, Charlie." She looked at him squarely. "It doesn't sound very good," she said gently.

"What doesn't sound very good?" came the enquiry from the kitchen door.

Adele let the note roll up, pushed it into her pocket, put a smile on her face and turned to the door. "Isa, you're up. Just in time for tea." She stood and gestured to her chair. "Toast and marmalade?"

Isa Hess was a woman of about Adele's age and height, but while Adele was dark haired, Isa had golden-white hair and fine

Aryan features, including crystalline blue eyes. She had been Adele's dearest friend when Adele had lived in Cape Town. Finding Isa standing at her front door two days ago had been a wonderful surprise. Adele had insisted Isa stay with her while she was in London, and had spent the last two days and evenings showing Isa her beloved city.

Isa slid onto the chair, yawning hard. She smiled at Charlie. "Hello."

Charlie didn't smile. "'ello."

"You aren't what I expected to find at the breakfast table." Isa's English was very good. She had barely any accent.

Charlie shrugged and picked up the glass of milk.

"This is Charlie, Isa." Adele slid a fresh cup and saucer in front of Isa, and set about toasting more bread.

"So, what doesn't sound very good, that you were talking about when I came in?" Isa asked Charlie.

Adele's heart leapt about as she tried to find an answer she could give Isa, before Charlie said anything.

Charlie gave another shrug. "Lady Adelaide don't like me sleepin' in the park." He scowled at Adele. "Keeps naggin' me to go t'the orphanage."

Adele focused on flipping the bread before it burned, while relief spread cool fingers through her middle.

"Oh dear, no, that does not sound very good at all," Isa said. "You are an orphan, Charlie?"

"Don't 'ave no mum or dad," Charlie said, his tone implying that he was disputing his status as an orphan.

"I see," Isa said diplomatically.

Charlie pushed the empty bread plate away from him and jumped up from the table. "May I go, my Lady?" His tone was polite, the question was what Adele had told him was the correct way to leave the table.

Adele would much rather have Charlie stay where he was, so

she could interview him more thoroughly, but she couldn't do that with Isa in the house. Reluctantly, she said, "Yes, Charlie. You may go. It was good to see you again."

"Thank you for the milk!" Charlie strained up on his toes to reach the high handle, and hauled the door open. He slipped out and the door shut again with a soft click.

Adele put the finished toast on a fresh plate, and put it in front of Isa. She took Charlie's chair and pulled her own barely touched toast toward her. She refilled her teacup and added milk.

"You are rather a dark horse, Adele," Isa said, picking up her own cup. "Here was I thinking you were the most proper English-woman I'd ever come across, while you are feeding homeless boys who come to your kitchen door."

Adele glanced at Isa's hair. When she had known Isa in the Cape Colony, her golden hair had been more than waist length, and worn in low chignon at the back of her head, in a similar fashion to the other matrons in their social circle.

Isa had since cut off her hair, so that it was now quite short, with waves that framed her face. It was a daring hairstyle few women had the courage to adopt, no matter how much they longed to be rid of their locks. Only the most fashionable women of the *ton* cut their hair—those who liked to take risks with their reputations.

Adele thought Isa was not in a good position to accuse Adele of impropriety. Adele lowered her cup. "It is only the one boy I feed, and he isn't here every day." She added, "He has an odd sense of what is appropriate," while thinking of the milk on her doorstep that he had *not* drunk, because it was hers. "Which reminds me. The newspaper will be at the front door. So will the mail." She got to her feet again. "I have kippers I can prepare, if you'd like something hot for breakfast?"

Isa grimaced and said in German. "Toast will do very well, thank you. After last night's dinner, I could forego eating for a week."

Adele collected the *Times* and her correspondence, and took them back to the little kitchen. The stove had warmed it marvelously. "Shall we stay here for the morning?" she suggested.

"I am quite happy to *not* move," Isa said firmly.

Adele handed her the paper. "I shall dress and be right back."

Upstairs in her bedroom, Adele withdrew the curled note from her pocket and re-examined it. It might be nothing, she told herself. But the long run of unbroken letters bothered her. Best to have Melville look at it, she decided. He would know if it was of any concern.

She changed, pushed the note into her skirt pocket, and went back downstairs.

Isa was deep into the *Times,* and had poured herself another cup of tea. Adele made more toast for herself, then pulled her correspondence over beside her plate and used a clean butter knife to open the letters.

She moved through them quickly, separating the letters she must answer at once from letters and invitations she wanted to mull over for a day or two. Melville liked her to attend as many society events as possible, but the Season had ended last month and few of the *ton* were left in London. She could take her time with the invitations and not risk offending anyone with a tardy response.

"'Phillip Cowden, Esquire'," Isa intoned. She lifted her gaze from the broadsheet. "Isn't that the silver-bearded man from last night?"

"Yes, indeed," Adele said. "It was a charity event. He was there to report upon it for the *Times*. Now the Season has ended, there's very little society news for him to write about."

Isa tapped the newspaper. "I was reading about the maiden voyage of this *HMS Lusitania*."

"Oh, yes, I forgot that she had been finished."

"It," Isa corrected her.

"*She*," Adele insisted, smiling. Sometimes, Isa's English slipped. So did Adele's German, but she had polished it a great deal in the last two days.

"This report says the *Lusitania* left on her maiden voyage to New York, yesterday. It was also written by Mr. Cowden."

"He is an energetic reporter," Adele replied. "I met him when we both attended the launch of the *Lusitania*, last year."

Isa lowered the newspaper. "And now you are associating with journalists, Adele?" Her brow lifted high.

Adele made herself give a small laugh. "He is a gentleman, even if he wasn't born to it."

Isa wrinkled her nose and laughed, too. "He was perfectly polite," she admitted and reached for her cup. "I was rather relieved when he interrupted the conversation with that poor widow..."

"Baroness Stroud," Adele replied. A small weight formed in her chest. The reason Lady Mary Stroud was a widow was because William Melville had shot her husband through the head, right in front of Adele, thereby stopping Stroud from assassinating the King of England. Mary Stroud would never know the truth about how her husband died. He had been buried with full honors befitting his rank as a peer of England. It made Adele's every social interaction with the widow almost painful, especially as Mary still wore mourning and had withdrawn from society for a full year.

"Yes, the Baroness," Isa said. "She seemed very insistent that you visit for afternoon tea today."

Adele lifted one of the letters by her plate. "I have a formal invitation here, for both of us."

"Oh, she really did mean for me to attend!" Isa was delighted.

"But I am afraid I have a prior engagement," Adele added.

Isa's face fell. "But...you said that you cancelled all your engagements, except for the interesting ones you wanted me to attend with you."

"I did. This came up rather suddenly."

Isa frowned, clearly casting about for a way to understand the sudden change of events.

The front doorbell clanged against the back wall. Adele got to her feet and hurried upstairs to answer it. The man in a white apron, holding a huge bunch of yellow roses, said, "Lady Adelaide Becket?"

"That is me," Adele told him, her heart pattering as she took in the glorious color of the blooms. She accepted them, thanked the man, and hurried back down to the kitchen with them.

Isa sat up, her brow lifting. "Oh, how *lovely!*" she cooed. "Who are they from? Will you tell me?"

"Leighton," Adele said, putting the card on the table where Isa could see it. There was no harm in letting Isa learn of a possible association between Daniel and her, for the roses were yellow. Their color meant that the careful check into Isa's background, her German antecedents and family connections, and her friends and associates, had uncovered nothing dangerous. Isa was merely a good friend who had stopped by to visit, as she had claimed.

If the roses had been red, though...

"Leighton?" Isa replied. "Oh, that lovely man, Daniel? The one with the eyes."

Adele smiled. "Yes, that one."

Isa opened the card. "It says nothing interesting." She seemed disappointed.

"That is because it is just a bouquet of roses, nothing more."

"At all?" Isa looked even more crestfallen.

"Isa, really! Hugh has only been dead for...for..."

"Two years in November," Isa said gently. "It isn't wrong for you to find a man's company interesting, Adele."

Adele could feel the small weight in her chest grow heavier. She had hated lying to Isa. The last two days had been tainted by the constant tension of wondering why Isa was here in London.

The roses had alleviated that tension, but now she felt guilty for having doubted Isa in the first place.

She got to her feet. "I will be late, if I do not leave immediately," she told Isa. "Please make yourself at home. I will return before lunch."

Isa opened her mouth—to protest, demand explanations, or even to ask where she had to go so early on a lazy Sunday morning. Adele avoided all of it by hurrying out of the room.

And her guilt twisted a little tighter.

WILLIAM MELVILLE'S FLAT WAS A typical bachelor's affair, with heavy, dark furniture more suited to last century's tastes, and minimal attempts to soften the sharp corners with cushions or cloth. Newspapers were everywhere, hanging over the arms of the sofa and the armchair, dropped onto the floor beside them, and abandoned upon the small table by the window, where the teapot sat amidst a small sea of dirty teacups, most of them without saucers.

Two men sprawled, Melville in the armchair, Torin Slane on the sofa. Both looked worse for wear, although it was difficult to discern details, for the drapes were still closed.

"Sundays are for rest," Adele said, as she closed the entrance door to the flat for herself. "But you are both taking it rather too far. There is a distinct odor in here..." She moved over to the window with determination.

"I've had very little sleep," Torin Slane muttered. "And my head is pounding—no, not the curtains!"

Adele ignored his cry and drew the curtains aside with sharp jerks on the heavy fabric. She tried to ignore the dust which swirled in the beams of bright sunlight which pierced the lace panels behind the drapes.

Slane hissed and winced and turned his head away from the light.

Melville made a h'rupping sound. "I suppose it is too much to

17

hope you brought breakfast with you?" His voice rose hopefully.

"As it is well past ten o'clock in the morning, no, I have not brought breakfast with me. But I do have a fruit cake." She brought the tin out of her basket and put it on the table.

Melville beamed at her. "You are a life-saver, Lady Adele."

Adele rolled her eyes, then turned to Slane. "What *are* you wearing, Mr. Slane?" His clothes reminded her of Charlie's garments. They were filthy, ripped and badly fitting. Slane's face was unshaved. His curly black hair flopped, unbrushed and unruly.

"Slane has been drifting about St. James's, watching Steinhauer," Melville supplied.

The rags were to make him look like a beggar, Adele realized. The homeless and poor folk who dared venture into the upper-class areas like St. James's were ignored by everyone but policemen. Workers going about their business were similarly not noticed. Melville used that tendency to good effect. He was excellent at hiding in plain sight, too. "For practice?" Adele asked, for Slane was new to Melville's odd business.

"And because I would like to know what the man is up to," Melville said.

"You are referring to Gustav Steinhauer, at the German Embassy?" Adele clarified, for Melville kept long lists of subjects of the Kaiser who resided in England, whose affairs he liked to monitor. "I thought Steinhauer was a friend of yours?"

"I would put him no higher than an acquaintance," Melville replied. "We met at Queen Victoria's funeral. He was guarding the Kaiser. I thought he was an American at first. His English is flawless."

"You liked him," Slane guessed, his eyes narrowed.

"What I feel about the man is irrelevant," Melville replied, with a shrug. "England must always come first."

Adele wished she had Melville's ability to disregard the loyalty one felt toward friends and family. Rather than let her thoughts return to that unhappy prospect, she pulled the note out of her pocket and put it in front of Melville. "What do you make of that?"

Melville spread the note out upon the arm of his chair. Slane moved along the sofa, so that he could bend his head to read it, too.

"Where did you get this?" Melville asked sharply.

Adele told them about Charlie as she opened the windows—which made Slane wince—then cut the cake with Melville's single kitchen knife. She placed pieces of the cake upon the cake tin lid and put the lid on the arm of the chair beneath the note they were studying.

"It's not a Caesar code," Melville muttered, as he tapped out letters on his knee, with all five fingers of the hand that didn't have a piece of cake in it.

"It will be in German," Adele pointed out.

Melville rolled his eyes at her.

Slane took a huge bite of his cake, and bent back over the slip of paper. "I t'ink…it might be a Vigenère." He looked at Melville triumphantly.

"You know codes, too?" Adele said, astonished. She had only just started to study them, at Melville's insistence.

Slane smiled. "I study history," he said. "And Vigenère is historical."

"So is the Caesar cypher," Melville pointed out.

Slane pushed the last of his piece of cake into his mouth, making his cheeks expand. He chewed mightily and swallowed as he got to his feet. He patted his pockets and looked around. "Pencil, pencil…why is there never a bleedin' pencil when you want one?"

"On the table," Adele pointed out.

"And paper!" Slane called, as he lunged for the table and snatched up the stub of a pencil lying there. He examined the point and tested it with his thumb.

"Melville's letterhead is in the drawer there," Adele said, pointing.

Melville looked at her sharply.

Slane withdrew a sheet of correspondence paper from the drawer in the tallboy, then moved back to the table. He shoved the newspapers aside. They fluttered to the floor.

Adele squeezed her hands into fists, to stop herself from moving to the table and picking up the errant newsprint. She would provide food, as that was the polite thing to do, but she would not tend to this room more than to make it comfortable for herself.

Instead, she picked up a slice of fruit cake and bit into it with her hand beneath to catch crumbs, while Slane scribbled furiously. He drew up a very large table, which filled most of the sheet. It had the letters of the alphabet across the top row and down the first side row.

"What is that?" Adele asked curiously.

"A *tabula recta*," Melville said softly, his tone admiring. He looked at her. "It helps solve the code."

Slane threw out his hand, his gaze upon the sheet of paper before him. "The note."

Adele held herself still. Calmly, she bit into her cake.

Slane then looked away from the sheet of paper. "Hand me the note," he repeated, his hand still out.

Adele chewed, enjoying the touch of ginger in the cake. The sultanas were sweet, too.

After a moment, Melville stirred, picked up the note and got to his feet so that he could lean and pass the note to Slane.

Slane took the note, his gaze on Adele.

She stared back.

Slane used two of the dirty teacups to spread the note and hold it flat. Then he took out a fresh sheet of paper and began to work.

"How long does it take?" Adele asked.

"It depends upon how complex the code is," Melville said.

"I see." She settled on the end of the sofa and withdrew the journal she was currently reading. *Annalen der Physik* was a German scientific publication, and this edition was nearly two years old. It was not her preferred reading, but Melville had strongly urged her to at least glance at one of the articles in it, entitled "On a Heuristic Viewpoint Concerning the Production and Transformation of Light" by a Herr Albert Einstein.

"You won't understand it," Melville told her as he had pushed the journal into her hands several days ago. "But you should study it anyway. This man will change science. You wait and see."

"And why do we need to concern ourselves with a scientist in Berlin?" Adele had asked, her tone cool.

"Science, my dear, will shape the war that is coming. The discoveries of scientists may well be the factor which decides who wins. But Einstein isn't a scientist. He's a patent clerk." He laughed at Adele's expression. "Which demonstrates that anyone may rise to whatever heights they wish, if they only apply themselves."

Adele had been attempting to read the article for several days now. Every line and every equation, nearly every word upon the page sent her scurrying for a dictionary, a science textbook, or both. She had spent an entire afternoon in the library, trying to make sense of the dense article. Analyzing every word and topic had introduced her to dozens of astounding ideas about the world around her, and the future itself. She had been utterly ignorant about so many subjects! Now she was slightly less ignorant and in awe of the man who had written the article.

Her notebook was stuffed full of notes to herself to investigate this or the other matter, when she was next in a library. It had been too long since she could indulge her curiosity among the shelves.

Some time later, Slane made a soft, pleased sound. "Damn it

t'hell, it's a Caesar, after all," he said, sitting back. "Crafty bugger, whoever it was. He rotated the number of letters by one letter… for every single letter." He shook his head.

Melville brushed his hands of crumbs and stood up. "That's a sort of Vigenère," he said.

"It's a twisty bit o' flummery," Slane admitted.

Adele put her journal away and moved over the table to see what Slane had deciphered. It was a single sentence.

Roastbeef zum Mittagessen.

Adele translated to English, aloud. "Dear Doctor; Roast beef for lunch."

"It is a prank," Melville said, disgusted.

"Not necessarily," Slane said. "The note was hidden in a bottle where anyone could pick it up."

"And someone did," Adele said.

"But not the right person," Slane said. "They've thought it t'roo. The milk bottle," and he pointed at the deciphered sentence, "plus a pre-arranged code. We just don't know what it means."

"And it could very well be neighbors issuing a luncheon invitation." Melville waved at the table dismissively.

"But it might not be," Adele said.

"And if it isn't, what should we do about it, hmm?" Melville asked her.

"Well, er…I'm not entirely sure."

"Exactly," Melville said. "There is too little here for us to act upon."

She could feel her shoulders slumping.

Melville gave her a grim smile. "If you come across the child again, you might ask him where he got it—"

"I did. He wouldn't tell me, because it is the scene of his crime. He stole the bottle."

"Well, then, there's nothing else to be done, is there?" Melville replied.

Or nothing that Melville wishes to do about it, Adele thought.

ADELE CLOSED THE DOOR OF her bedroom very quietly, and moved along the corridor and down the stairs, clinging to the sides of the steps where there was less chance they would squeak.

Isa sat in Adele's armchair, reading. The lamp next to her was turned low and sat so the small light fell upon the pages of her book. She looked up.

Adele silently cursed and stepped down the last step.

Isa's eyes widened comically. "Good Lord above, Adele! Whatever are you wearing?" She put the book aside and got to her feet. "You look positively reprehensible."

Adele tugged at the stained, torn dress and tried to resist the need to tuck the flyaway ends of her hair back into a neater knot on the back of her head. She pulled the shawl in around her to hide that she was not wearing a corset. She had picked at the wool in the shawl for twenty minutes, creating snags and runs, before grinding the wool into the ashes on the hearth of the fireplace in her bedroom. "I was attempting to look homeless and pathetic," she admitted. "But reprehensible will do, I suppose."

"Your spine is too straight for pathos," Isa decided. Her eyes twinkled. "Whatever you are up to, it sounds like enormous fun. Do let me come with you! I can tear up a dress, too."

Adele shook her head. "I'm sorry, Isa. I can't allow that. To-night is not an evening of diversions."

Isa's smile faded. "Then what is it?" she demanded.

"I can't say," Adele said. "At least, not right now." It was only a small white lie, she told herself.

The implication that she would tell Isa everything at some un-specified later date mollified her friend. Isa sighed. "You will tell me absolutely everything?" she insisted. "Honestly, Adele, I had no idea you had such an exotic nature!"

Adele grimaced and managed to turn it into a smile. "I must away."

Isa stood aside, her smile returning. "*So* mysterious!"

IT TOOK TWO HOURS TO walk to Spa Fields, on the northern edges of Clerkenwell, as no cab driver would consent to taking Adele anywhere, even if she paid him first. Instead, she told herself the exercise would be beneficial.

She kept her shoulders hunched in and the shawl around her head, and stayed in the shadows as much as possible. She slipped through the gates of the park just after midnight, which suited her. By midnight, even the most restless of souls would be deeply asleep.

The park was oddly-shaped, with a thick copse of trees in the center. Instinctively, Adele moved toward the dark shadows beneath them. Even before she reached the trees, the shadows shifted and stirred.

As she stepped beneath the late summer canopy of leaves, a voice hissed, "Bugger off, missus, this 'ere's our place."

Adele halted. "I'm looking for Charlie Rowbottom." She coarsened her accent. "'ave yer seen him? I've got a message for 'im."

Silence.

Now she was away from the street lamps for a few minutes, her eyes had adjusted. The smaller shadows beneath the trees developed details. Four boys, all curled up between the big roots of the oak. They had pushed dried leaves from previous summers over themselves, for warmth.

Her throat closed over.

"Don't know 'oo yer talking about," one of them muttered.

"Thar's a rich lady, over by 'yde Park, says she 'as something for Charlie. She gave me a bob, too." Money might entice them to be more forthcoming.

The silence built for a moment, then one of them whispered,

"Clay…?"

"*Shut yer gob*!" came the furious rejoinder.

"Clay?" Adele repeated. "You know Charlie, then?"

One of the larger lads, farthest from Adele, leapt to his feet and ran. Adele cursed, jumped over the feet of those still beneath the tree, and ran after him, thanking the heavens that she'd left her corset off.

Clay had long legs, but so did Adele. She pursued him across a large swathe of open grass. Ahead were more trees and the outline of buildings. The glow of gas lamps indicated a street lay ahead.

Adele gritted her teeth and ran faster. She caught the boy as he reached the shadows of the trees edging this side of the park and they both went down and rolled. She held onto Clay's jacket with a firm grip and sat up.

Clay had dirty blonde hair and dirt on his face, but she could see little else in the moonless night. She gave him a shake. "I intend no harm toward Charlie, but you must tell me where he is. It is very important, Clay. He might be in serious trouble."

Clay gave a choking sound and hung his head. "Charlie's dead."

Adele drew in a sharp breath. "No, that's not possible—he was fine this morning…"

Clay's shoulders gave a hitch. Then he wiped his sleeve across his eyes, gave a mighty sniff. "You're the rich lady, ain't yer?"

"I'm the lady from Hyde Park, more or less," Adele told him, her heart aching. "But I'm not rich. Charlie really is dead, Clay?"

Clay nodded, his shoulders still hunched. "They found 'im this afternoon, in a passage off Woodbridge. Someone dun 'im in."

Adele's chest ached. "How did they do it, Clay? Do you know?"

"Don't know. Coppers say 'e starved. Just curled up 'is toes 'n gave up. But Charlie wozn't like that…"

"No, he wasn't at all like that," Adele said in agreement. The lack of obvious wounds meant no gun or knife had been involved. Had they strangled Charlie? Broken his neck? A broken neck was usually obvious, too, but the police might have chosen to overlook it in order to close the matter quickly and get on with their day. "I'll find out what happened," Adele told Clay. "I promise you I'll find who did it."

"You think someone did for 'im, too, then?"

"I suspect that is the case, yes. That is what I want to find out. Where is Woodbridge Street?" She got to her feet, bent and retrieved her shawl from where she had dropped it.

Clay pointed. "Starts right at the corner of the park," he added. "Folk on that street, they order cream, sometimes."

The location of the street seemed to fit with the little she knew of Charlie's habits, and if the street was known for generous orders to the milkman, it made even more sense that Charlie had been found there.

Adele pulled her shawl around her shoulders once more. "Go back to your bed. I shan't bother you any more tonight."

Clay got slowly to his feet. "Coppers say 'e'll get a pauper's grave." Anger lay behind the words, buried deep.

"I'll look into it," she promised him. "I'll find out where he is buried, at least, so you can visit, if you want."

"Don't care," Clay said sullenly. "Doesn't matter."

"It is *does* matter, Clay." She rested her hand briefly against his shoulder, then headed for the corner of the park to where he had pointed. Woodbridge Street was directly opposite the park, just as Clay had said, and she relaxed a little. He hadn't sent her on a wild goose chase, after all.

But it was still deep in the middle of the night and the lack of moon wouldn't help her discern any details. Woodbridge Street was lit by only three gas lamps along its entire length, that she could see, and even they would be extinguished in the next hour.

She turned to look behind her. The trees at this end of the park were few, and the ground between filled in with bushes which looked thorny. Adele returned to the nearest tree with a canopy that didn't brush the ground. Old, dried berries cracked under her boots. Adele brushed the ground clear of them, right against the trunk and settled with her back against it and listened to the traffic on far streets. There was little of it. Horses clopped and occasionally, a motor car engine puttered. Most of the city, though, was fast asleep.

She woke to weak first light and the chitter of larks...and a light tapping against her shoulder.

Adele looked up, blinking. A police constable stood over her. It was his truncheon against her arm which had woken her.

He straightened and put his thumbs into his belt and curled his fingers over it. "Time to move off, luv. Yer done for the night. Clear?"

Adele attempted to rise to her feet, but found she was stiff and sore and damp. She used the trunk to pull herself up, and wrapped the shawl around her, shivering.

All through the trees of the park, she could see other police officers bending and stirring those who had slept beyond dawn.

"Sorry, sir," Adele said. "I'll be on me way, like."

"See that you do," the policeman said. He moved off without waiting to see she obeyed. He used his truncheon to push back the prickly branches of the bushes, to check beneath.

Adele moved out to the footpath and put her shawl over her head and wrapped it about her closely, for the morning was damp and cool. She crossed the street and moved down Woodbridge Street. The light was enough to see details, now. She shuffled slowly down the footpath on the southwest side of the street, keeping her back bent, and examined every front door she passed.

All of them had milk bottle holders sitting upon the step, all holding one or more empty milk bottles. She noted the details of each door and bottle holder, but none of them held a bottle which appeared to be full of milk.

At the far end of the street, Adele crossed to the other side and walked slowly back in the other direction, examining doors and bottles. She was halfway down the street and the daylight was full, when she saw a milkman's cart turn into the street, the horse plodding with habitual slowness. Two men carried bottles over to the doors, brought back empty bottles to drop into the cart, pick up full bottles and repeated the cycle.

Adele quickened her step, checking the doors as she passed them. She slid past the milkman working this side of the street. None of the bottle holders would tell her anything, now, for they all held fresh milk. But she took note of the few which were left.

Nothing seemed out of place. Nothing odd beckoned for her attention.

Adele turned once more and moved back down Woodbridge Street, for her house lay in that direction. As she reached the end of the street, another cart came around the corner. The baker's cart.

A man with grey hair sat upon the side of the cart, preparing to jump off so he could deliver his loaves to the houses. He paused when he saw her. Adele turned her head away, hiding behind the edge of the shawl.

"Hey! Luv!"

She glanced back, peering around the edge of the shawl.

The baker tossed her a small bun. She got her hand up and caught it, then stared at him.

"Shh!" he said, and winked. Then he hopped off the cart and picked up an armful of loaves wrapped in paper and headed for the nearest house.

Adele got moving once more, and tore at the bun, which was still warm from the oven and thick with raisins. It was possibly one of the best breakfasts she'd ever eaten.

ADELE DEVOTED THE REST OF her day to entertaining Isa. They strolled to the markets, shopped for gloves and hats, and visited Adele's dressmaker. They walked through Hyde Park, and took afternoon tea at Brown's Hotel.

That evening, Adele served dinner in her tiny dining room and they gossiped about the people they had known in the Cape Colony, and what they were up to now. And because Adele was exhausted from her energetic night and uncomfortable bed under the trees, she went to bed early.

She also wound up her alarm clock, and set it for several hours before dawn. Instead of leaving it sitting upon her bedside table, she put the clock under her pillow, which would muffle the alarm and avoid waking Isa.

It was just past three in the morning when Adele eased out of her room, wearing the clothes she had worn last night. Now the ragged dress bore genuine dirt and wear, and was beginning to smell quite authentic.

Isa opened the door of her bedroom as Adele passed.

"Oh, my dear God, Isa!" Adele hissed, her heart hammering. "What are you doing awake at this hour?"

"Your alarm clock woke me," Isa said, pulling her wrapper in around her. "You used an alarm to wake yourself in the middle of the night, when you haven't used one at all since I arrived. What on earth is going on?"

"I can't tell you that," Adele said.

"You said you would tell me later."

"Later than this," Adele prevaricated. "I really must go." She had to be on Woodbridge Street long before the milkman got there. She barely had time as it was.

As she turned to go, Isa caught her arm. "Are you in trouble, Adele? Is that what this is? Are you...earning money in some strange way?"

"Good grief, no!" Adele shot back, genuinely startled.

Relief showed in Isa's face. "Then tell me what you are doing. Maybe I can help."

"You can't help with this," Adele assured her. "This is something I must do myself."

"And you won't tell me what it is?"

"I cannot," Adele said, the weight in her chest growing harder and heavier. "I wish I could," she added honestly.

Isa's face closed over. "I am beginning to think I do not know you very well at all, Adelaide Becket."

Time! Time! The litany nagged her. Adele grimaced. "I'm sorry, but we must discuss this later, Isa. I simply *must* go."

She pulled her arm from Isa's grip and hurried down the stairs, feeling sick and hot from the jumping in her middle and the squeezing in her chest.

ADELE ARRIVED AT THE SOUTHERNMOST end of Woodbridge Street well before dawn. This time she did not shuffle along as she had yesterday morning. A full bottle of milk would stand out among empty bottles, even on a dark night like this, for her eyes had become accustomed to the low light on the walk from Mayfair.

As she moved up the street, examining every doorstep, she marveled upon how man was a creature of habit. The milk holders were in exactly the same place as they had been yesterday. Some houses put theirs to the left of the door, some to the right. Some turned theirs sideways, to leave more room for passage through the doorway. Some didn't.

No one put their milk bottle holder in the middle of the doorway.

Adele found the milk bottle which appeared to be full almost halfway down the street. The white bottle sat in the back corner of the bottle holder, half hidden by the empty containers around it.

Adele glanced up at the house, startled to have found what

she was looking for. Her heart beat heavily. She missed a step and stumbled a little. Breathing hard, she crossed the street to the house directly opposite the one with the full bottle of milk in their bottle holder. There, she borrowed Charlie's habit. She sank to the doorstep and put her back to the door. She pulled her shawl in around her so the paleness of her face was mostly hidden and examined the door across the way.

What was different about the house, apart from the milk? She had examined it just yesterday morning. What did studying it tell her now? Melville would have been able to give her the number of people living in the house and the likely occupation of the father, in a single sweeping glance.

Adele's gaze settled on the window. Her heart leapt again.

The lavender! That was what was different. A pot of lavender sat precisely in the middle of the windowsill. It had not been there yesterday. To Adele's gaze, the pot was too big for the sill and jutted out into the room, which also pushed the lace curtains out.

It looked awkward there. Had it been Adele's pot of lavender, she would have found another place for it. The household clearly had a woman's touch, as told by the lace curtains. Melville's lace curtains had been installed by his landlady. Would this house's lady allow an oversized pot to ruin the hang of the curtains the way it was?

Adele came back to the single fact that supported her suspicions: The pot had not been there yesterday morning. It was a signal.

She saw the man before she heard him, for he was moving very quietly. His hat and his suit were dark and he wore a scarf and overcoat which hid any touch of white, including his collar. Only his face was unshadowed, the flesh white above an unshaved jaw. He strolled as if it was not indecently early and he did not look at the houses he was passing. He was on the other side of the road from Adele.

She held her breath and pulled the shawl in closely around her face, trying to shrink back into the corner of the doorway. He could live in one of the houses on this street, or nearby, and was using this street to reach an underground train station. There were all sorts of reasons why he might be walking along the street at this unusual hour.

She held her breath as he drew close to the house with lavender in the window. It was still too dark to see if he looked at the window himself. Then he turned in between the iron railings at the front of the house, bent and plucked the milk bottle from the holder and slid it inside his coat, turned and moved down the path once more.

The whole motion took only three or four seconds, during which Adele's thoughts held still, just like her breath.

Yes, I saw him take the bottle, she told herself firmly. It had happened so fast! He had not hesitated, or looked around furtively. He hadn't even glanced in her direction. When he had turned toward the door, it had looked like the most natural thing in the world...so much so, that for a moment she thought the man really did live there.

Her surprise kept her sitting on the doorstep long enough for the man to draw several yards ahead of her. Adele rose to her feet and moved down the street after him, staying on her side. As he approached the end of Woodbridge Street, Adele hurried her pace, closing the distance between them, so she would not miss the direction he took.

Instead, the man turned a sharp angle to the right and disappeared.

Alarmed, Adele hurried to catch up with him, to see where he had turned in. There was a narrow lane, barely wide enough for a horse and cart to go through. The yards of houses facing in the other direction backed onto the lane.

The man was nowhere to be seen.

Her heart thudding, Adele walked swiftly along the lane. She could see a corner not far ahead. He might be around that.

As she passed one of the yards, a shadow rose from behind the chest-high wall. The man reached over and grabbed her right arm and pulled her toward him.

Adele slammed into the wall, all her breath shoved out of her. The man's hand reached for her face, but his fingers snagged on her shawl. Adele reared back, pushing against the wall with her other hand.

The man was strong and kept pulling at her. Eventually, he would pull her right over the wall. She suspected that what happened to Charlie would then happen to her. Had he been reaching for her throat, like he had with Charlie?

She weighed her options, as she fought to push back off the wall and tear her arm out of his grip. In a few seconds, her strength would run out.

Adele curled her left hand into a fist, raised it and stopped tugging backwards. She was yanked forward to slam against the wall once more, but this time she was braced for it. She punched the man directly on the bridge of his nose. Flying up against the wall gave her punch extra strength.

"*Bloede Kuh!*" the man muttered, as blood spurted from his nose and dripped into the dark scarf. Yet his grip on her arm did not loosen. He was pulling her up the wall and would pull her right over the top of it in a moment or two.

Adele put her hands on the top of the wall and jumped up so that she was leaning over it. Then she reached and grasped the back of his head with both hands and jerked his head forward and downward. He was blinded by the punch to the nose and didn't see the wall. His head rammed into it and he fell back, staggering, then dropped to his knees, his hands to his face.

Adele hung over the top of the wall with her mouth open, astonished at how effectively she had fought him off.

In the two heart beats she hung on the wall, she weighed up her options and came to a swift decision. While the man breathed noisily, making little sounds of pain, Adele pushed herself off the wall, brushed off her hands, picked up her shawl and ran as if the devil was on her heels.

MELVILLE DIDN'T DISMISS HER, THIS time. While Adele recovered her breath, he roused Torin Slane, who emerged from the small guest bedroom only a few minutes later in a perfectly proper suit, and hurried out the door.

"Slane will rouse Leighton," Melville said. "They'll find out what they can about the house with the lavender. We'll work it back from that end. Now, tell me everything again, from the very beginning."

Adele recounted her activities of the last two days, including Charlie's death, and Isa's irritation with her. As she related all of it, she could feel her discomfort rising at the reminder of the constant lies she was telling her friends these days.

At the end of her account, Melville smoothed out his moustache with a flick of his finger. "This might have all come out right if you had not rushed off to take care of things all by yourself." His tone sounded urbane, but Adele could hear the irritation in it.

"But you *told* me to take care of it myself!" she protested.

"I did no such thing," Melville replied.

"You said 'If you come across the child again, you might ask him where he got it'."

"Which you said you had already asked—" Melville halted and held up his hand. "There is no point arguing this. The thing is done. Now we must adjust as best we can and see if we can't make this come out right."

"Why *shouldn't* I act upon my own accord?" Adele demanded. "You were certainly not interested in pursuing the matter. And now, you see, my instincts were right. There *is* more to this than neighbors dining upon roast beef."

"By striking out on your own you have thoroughly messed things up," Melville shot back. "If you had told me about this even yesterday afternoon, we could have been there to follow the man this morning, *and* got the contents of the milk bottle, too."

"You don't need the contents of the milk bottle to know what it is!" Adele shot back. "Clearly, the first note went missing, because Charlie took it. The message this morning will be the same—a repetition, for the right man to receive."

Melville stared at her. Then he muttered something she could not hear.

"I beg your pardon?" she asked, her tone chilly.

"I said, I suppose you might be right. On *that* point at least."

Adele glared at him. "You are a sore loser, Melville. And I thought more highly of you than that."

His mouth dropped open.

Adele got to her feet, her emotions too jangled to remain seated. "How do you *stand* it? The lying, the hiding, the…the… creeping about? Never being able to explain all your oddities to your friends? My most dearest friend, the woman who made my time in the Cape Colony bearable, is in my house right now, sure that my soul is in mortal danger, and disappointed because I will not tell her the truth about any of this. How do you do it?"

Melville drew in a breath. "I suppose…I do not have friends." And he grimaced.

"You have acquaintances, whom you do not trust."

"I realize that this might be hard on you, Lady Adele, but you must think of the greater good. Of England. And…" Melville gave her a little smile, "You *are* rather good at the work."

"Oh!" Adele said softly. "That still doesn't help me deal with Isa. Or the rest of society. I grew up with most of the people of the *ton*, and now I must hide most of my true life from them and pretend to be something I'm not. I can barely look Baroness

Stroud in the eye, these days."

Melville's gaze skittered away from hers. He looked around the room desperately. "Let me make you a cup of tea, my lady."

Adele sighed. "Very well. Thank you. But…may I wash the cup out first?"

WHEN SLANE HAD NOT RETURNED two hours later, Adele got up from Melville's sofa and pronounced that she was going home to take care of her guest and that Melville could find her there.

She hurried back to her house, hoping to return before Isa came downstairs. Adele hoped she could get upstairs without being seen, to wash and put on her real clothes.

But Isa was sitting in the wing chair in the corner of the drawing room, the chair which faced the front door. Placed in front of her were the two new style suit-cases she had arrived with.

Adele took in Isa's coat, the gloves sitting on the arm of the chair and the hat upon the table beside her. "Oh, Isa…"

Isa shook her head. "You don't have to explain. I'd rather you didn't. I can't think of many things which require a lady to dress as you are, two nights in a row, and to leave the house for hours on end. Every explanation I can think of would cause me to re-examine our friendship, if it were the real explanation. And I really think that if I pressed you for the truth, you might feel it necessary to *not* be truthful and that, I could not bear at all."

"Neither could I," Adele said flatly. She sighed. "I don't want to lose our friendship."

"As I feel the same, I must leave," Isa said softly. She got to her feet.

"Shall I hail a cab for you? There are usually two or three just around the corner."

"Looking as you do? I rather think I will have better luck, even with my accent." Isa put on her coat as she spoke. "I will walk around the corner, and find one myself. I was planning to do that, but I wanted to wait for you to come back home. I wanted to speak to you first. It did not feel right to simply leave without explanation and a letter would not do." She slipped her hat on, which was made much simpler because her hair was cut short and she had no buns or chignons to ease beneath it. Nor did she bother with a hat pin. "I've done a great deal of thinking, sitting here," Isa continued. "Mostly, I have been thinking about the time we knew each other in Cape Town, after the war."

"They were happier times," Adele admitted.

"Were they?" Isa glanced at her. "Hugh was importing dry goods, yes?"

"Yes, for all the retailers in Cape Town. He was very good at it."

"Mmm…" Isa slid her gloves on and fussed with the fit over her fingers. "People still talk about Hugh Becket, you know. Everyone liked him. He got on with simply everybody."

"Yes, Hugh was rather good at getting along with people," Adele replied. Her heart was hurting. In the three days Isa had been here, this was the first time she had spoken about Hugh, or referred to the Boer War where her own husband had been killed.

"That was what I was recalling, along with some rumors that…well…if those rumors were true, then that would make Hugh a person with secrets just as you have been since I arrived here."

Adele grew still. "What do you mean, Isa?"

Isa picked up her reticule and threaded the handle over her forearm. "I mean the rumors that your husband was really an agent for the British government, reporting back to them on us Germans."

Adele could feel the shock curling up through her toes, to numb her knees and her fingers and finally, her lips. "An…agent?"

"It would certainly explain the other rumor, the one about your house catching fire not being an accident, wouldn't it?" Isa picked up her suit-cases, one per hand. "Would you mind opening the door for me, dear friend?"

Adele made herself move. She unlatched the door and opened it wide. "Isa..." A thousand questions pushed at her, but she could voice none of them, because to do so would reveal that she knew far more about the business of agents and spies than she should.

Isa leaned over the suit-case in her hand and brushed her lips against Adele's cheek. "Be well, Lady Adelaide."

Then she was gone.

WHAT FINALLY FORCED ADELE TO move was the stench rising from the horrid dress she was wearing. She lifted herself up from the bottom step and went upstairs to bathe and change. The act of moving helped her sluggish mind move, too.

When she was finally clean, Adele took her homeless clothing down to the kitchen and burnt them in the stove.

As the last fragment of cotton turned to ash, Adele realized her belly was very empty. Even though she did not want to eat, she prepared toast and tea and made herself eat and drink.

Afterward, she collected her letters and settled at the secretary to catch up on her correspondence, which helped her mind stop its ceaseless circling and questioning. When every letter and invitation had been answered, Adele picked a book from her shelves—Lewis Carroll, this time—and sat in the chair by the fire to distract herself.

Melville, Slane and Daniel arrived shortly after two o'clock that afternoon. The three of them in her tiny drawing room made her feel much as Alice must have after eating the cake marked "Eat Me" and finding herself unable to fit into the house. There was too little room with the four of them there at once.

"I'll make tea," Adele declared and led them down to her larger kitchen, with the big worktable. She pulled the bench she used to reach the upper shelves over to the table for two of them to use. "You look as though you are brimming with news," she added, as she built up the stove fire once more.

"Leighton insisted we tell you of what happened," Melville said. From the corner of her eye, Adele saw him reach for an apple in the bowl on the table.

"It all happened so quickly," Slane added. "T'ank the Lord you came straight round to tell us about the lavender business, Lady Adelaide. We'd not have been watching the house when the man left, otherwise."

"Perhaps you should start at the beginning," Adele suggested.

"The master of the house with the lavender on the sill was Johann Simons," Daniel said. "He was a minor clerk employed by an industrial company in Clerkenwell, and their business is neither secret, nor sensitive. Simons was an exemplary worker. He was never ill, he worked hard and took one week a year off to take his family on a holiday. This year, he took them to Brighton."

Adele sat on the only remaining chair. "The man sounds perfectly innocent, except for the name."

Melville nodded, as he chewed swiftly so he could speak.

"Ye'd expect so, hearin' that, wouldn't ye?" Slane said, instead. "So did we, right up until he left his office and walk to St. James's Church Garden. Then he bally well sits down and eats a sandwich and reads!"

Adele blinked, bewildered. "Because eating a picnic lunch in a church garden is against the law?"

"The Irishman is leaving out a detail or two," Daniel said smoothly. Slane shot him a scowl, which he ignored. "Including the very important detail that when he returned to his office for the afternoon, he left the book sitting on the bench."

Adele caught her breath. "Someone picked it up?"

Daniel's smile was rich and full of warmth that reached his eyes. "Very good. Yes. Someone with two black eyes and a ferocious cut upon his forehead sat upon the bench, picked up the book and read it. Then, two minutes later, he left. He took the book with him."

"You got *both* of them!" Adele said to Melville, delighted.

"Aye, yes, we did," Melville admitted.

She leaned forward. "What was in the book? Something larger than could fit in the milk bottle, or too valuable to risk leaving in the bottle, which is why they had to meet somewhere else. *Roast Beef for lunch* was a code telling the receiving agent where and when they should meet."

Daniel's smile grew. "You tumbled to it first try. Melville had to explain it to me."

"The book was hollow, the middle cut out of all the pages," Melville said.

"Damn waste of a good book," Slane muttered darkly.

"It was Yeats," Daniel pointed out.

"I rest my case," Slane shot back.

"What was in it?" Adele repeated to Melville.

Melville sighed.

"A stack of papers and photographs of documents, people and ships," Daniel said. "All of them observations on the *HMS Dreadnought*. Specifications, armaments, personnel, sail dates and itineraries…if the Germans had got hold of that, they'd know exactly where to place their torpedoes and when to do it."

"Taking down the *Dreadnought* would be a damned blow to England," Melville added.

"I've heard naval officers at soirees sigh over the magnificence of the *Dreadnought*," Adele admitted. "Most of them say the ship's design and performance is far beyond that of any military vessel previously built. That she will change naval history."

"And she will, as long as she continues to sail," Melville said. "Thanks to you, Lady Adele, she *will* continue to sail."

Adele frowned. "But how did a clerk in a warehouse in Clerkenwell obtain that sort of information?"

Daniel shook his head. "In all the Seasons you have attended, you've never visited Brighton, Adele?"

She shook her head. "There was never time. Then I met Hugh and…" Isa's parting words about her husband's possible secrets came back to her. "No, I've never been to Brighton," she said flatly.

"Brighton is just a wee bit up the road from Portsmouth," Slane said. "A man could easily leave his family at the beach at Brighton and spend the day in Portsmouth, taking notes and watching all the comings and goings. Perhaps, even an ale at the local inn where the sailors drink, where he could buy an officer lunch while they chatted, all chummy and sociable."

The kettle began to steam. Daniel got to his feet, picked up the tea towel and hooked the kettle off the stove, then carefully filled the teapot. Adele beamed at him.

"This affair today," Melville said, his tone didactic, "demonstrates that these agents are recruiting every-day Germans already living here in England to do their dirty work for them. Johann Simons came to England as a boy, with his parents. It is no longer sufficient for us to look for strangers and newcomers to a community. We need to look at everyone, question everyone and trust no one."

Adele gripped her hands together. "As you trust no one, Melville?"

"Yes," he said harshly.

She squeezed her hands together. "I trust everyone sitting at this table," she said flatly.

"We barely know Slane," Daniel pointed out.

Slane glared at him again.

"And because I trust everyone at this table," Adele continued, lifting her voice, "I will ask you, Melville, in front of everyone." She swallowed. "Was my husband your agent in the Cape Colony?"

Daniel gasped.

"Is that why my husband and my son were murdered, Melville?" Adele said.

Daniel shifted on the bench to look squarely at Melville.

So did Slane.

Melville took his time answering. He smoothed out his moustache. Then he reached into his jacket and withdrew a slip of paper. This note was folded. He put it on the table and slid it in front of Adele.

"What is that?"

"The lot number in which Charlie Rowbottom will be buried later today."

Adele's eyes prickled with tears and she blinked hard to disperse them as she stared at the note.

"You asked me, this morning, Lady Adele," Melville continued, "about how I withstand the pressure of lying to everyone dear to me. I told you I had no friends to care about lying to, and that is nearly true. The real truth, though, is on that note in front of you."

Adele looked up at him, puzzled.

Melville gave a small shrug. "I do this work for all the people who cannot speak or act, who have lost their voice or their freedom, because of the deeds of Germans like Simons and his contact, and the German who killed Slane's brother, and the Germans who stole a young debutante's life. I do this work for people like Charlie. Remembering that makes lying to friends easier to bear."

Adele sighed. He wouldn't answer her, because he didn't want to lie to her. She picked up the note. "I understand," she said heavily. "Thank you, Melville."

He nodded and reached for another apple.

About the Author

Tracy Cooper-Posey is a #1 Best Selling Author. She writes romantic suspense, historical, paranormal and science fiction romance. She has published over 100 novels since 1999, been nominated for five CAPAs including Favourite Author, and won the Emma Darcy Award.

She turned to indie publishing in 2011. Her indie titles have been nominated four times for Book Of The Year. Tracy won the award in 2012, and a SFR Galaxy Award in 2016 for "Most Intriguing Philosophical/Social Science Questions in Galaxybuilding" She has been a national magazine editor and for a decade she taught romance writing at MacEwan University.

She is addicted to Irish Breakfast tea and chocolate, sometimes taken together. In her spare time she enjoys history, Sherlock Holmes, science fiction and ignoring her treadmill. An Australian Canadian, she lives in Edmonton, Canada with her husband, a former professional wrestler, where she moved in 1996 after meeting him on-line.

Did you enjoy this book?

How to make a big difference!

Reviews are *powerful.*

Authors like me, without the financial muscle of a sleek New York publisher backing me, can't take advertisements out in the subways and billboards of the world.

On the other hand, New York publishers would *kill* to get what I have: A committed and loyal group of readers.

Honest reviews of my books help bring them to the attention of other readers. If you enjoyed this book I would be grateful if you could spend just a few minutes leaving a review (it can be as short as you like) on the book's page where you bought it.

Thank you so much!

Tracy

Other books by
Tracy Cooper-Posey

For reviews, excerpts, and more about each title, visit Tracy's site and click on the cover you are interested in: http://tracycooperposey.com/books-by-thumbnail/

Adelaide Becket

(Historical Suspense Series)
The Requisite Courage
The Rosewater Debutante
The Unaccompanied Widow
The Lavender Semaphore

Scandalous Scions

(Historical Romance Series – Spin off)
Rose of Ebony
Soul of Sin
Valor of Love
Marriage of Lies
Scandalous Scions One (Boxed Set)
Mask of Nobility
Law of Attraction
Veil of Honor
Scandalous Scions Two (Boxed Set)
Season of Denial
Rules of Engagement
Degree of Solitude
Ashes of Pride
Risk of Ruin

Year of Folly
Queen of Hearts

Scandalous Families – The Victorians

(Historical Romance Series – Spin off)
His Parisian Mistress
Her Rebellious Prince
Their Foreign Affair

Once and Future Hearts

(Ancient Historical Romance—Arthurian)
Born of No Man
Dragon Kin
Pendragon Rises
War Duke of Britain
High King of Britain
Battle of Mount Badon
Abduction of Guenivere
Downfall of Cornwall
Vengeance of Arthur
Grace of Lancelot
The Grail and Glory
Camlann

Kiss Across Time Series

(Paranormal Time Travel)
Kiss Across Time
Kiss Across Swords
Time Kissed Moments
Kiss Across Chains
Kiss Across Time Box One (Boxed Set)
Kiss Across Deserts
Kiss Across Kingdoms
Time and Tyra Again
Kiss Across Seas
Kiss Across Time Box Two (Boxed Set)

Kiss Across Worlds
Time and Remembrance
Kiss Across Tomorrow
More Time Kissed Moments
Kiss Across Blades
Kiss Across Chaos

Project Kobra

(Romantic Spy Thrillers)
Hunting The Kobra
Inside Man
Heart Strike

Blood Knot Series

(Urban Fantasy Paranormal Series)
Blood Knot
Southampton Swindle
Broken Promise
Vale
Amor Meus
Blood Stone
Blood Unleashed
Blood Drive
Blood Revealed
Blood Ascendant
Flesh + Blood (Boxed Set)

Vistaria Has Fallen

Vistaria Has Fallen
Prisoner of War
Hostage Crisis
Freedom Fighters
Casualties of War
V-Day
The Vistaria Affair (Boxed Set)

Romantic Thrillers Series

Fatal Wild Child
Dead Again
Dead Double
Terror Stash
Thrilling Affair (Boxed Set)

Beloved Bloody Time Series

(Paranormal Futuristic Time Travel)
Bannockburn Binding
Wait
Byzantine Heartbreak
Viennese Agreement
Romani Armada
Spartan Resistance
Celtic Crossing
Beloved Bloody Time Series Boxed Set

Scandalous Sirens

(Historical Romance Series)
Forbidden
Dangerous Beauty
Perilous Princess

Go-get-'em Women

(Short Romantic Suspense Series)
The Royal Talisman
Delly's Last Night
Vivian's Return
Ningaloo Nights

The Sherlock Holmes Series

(Romantic Suspense/Mystery)
Chronicles of the Lost Years
The Case of the Reluctant Agent
Sherlock Boxed In

The Kine Prophecies

(Epic Norse Fantasy Romance)
The Branded Rose Prophecy

The Stonebrood Saga

(Gargoyle Paranormal Series)
Carson's Night
Beauty's Beasts
Harvest of Holidays
Unbearable
Sabrina's Clan
Pay The Ferryman
Hearts of Stone (Boxed Set)

Destiny's Trinities

(Urban Fantasy Romance Series)
Beth's Acceptance
Mia's Return
Sera's Gift
The First Trinity
Cora's Secret
Zoe's Blockade
Octavia's War
The Second Trinity
Terra's Victory
Destiny's Trinities (Boxed Set)

Interspace Origins

(Science Fiction Romance Series)
Faring Soul
Varkan Rise
Cat and Company
Interspace Origins (Boxed Set)

Short Paranormals

Solstice Surrender
Eva's Last Dance
Three Taps, Then....
The Well of Rnomath

Jewels of Tomorrow

(Historical Romantic Suspense)
Diana By The Moon
Heart of Vengeance

The Endurance

(Science Fiction Romance Series)
5,001
Greyson's Doom
Yesterday's Legacy
Promissory Note
Quiver and Crave
Xenogenesis
Junkyard Heroes
Evangeliya
Skinwalker's Bane

Contemporary Romances

Lucifer's Lover
An Inconvenient Lover
Contemporary Romances Boxed Set

Non-Fiction Titles

Reading Order

(Non-Fiction, Reference)
Reading Order Perpetual